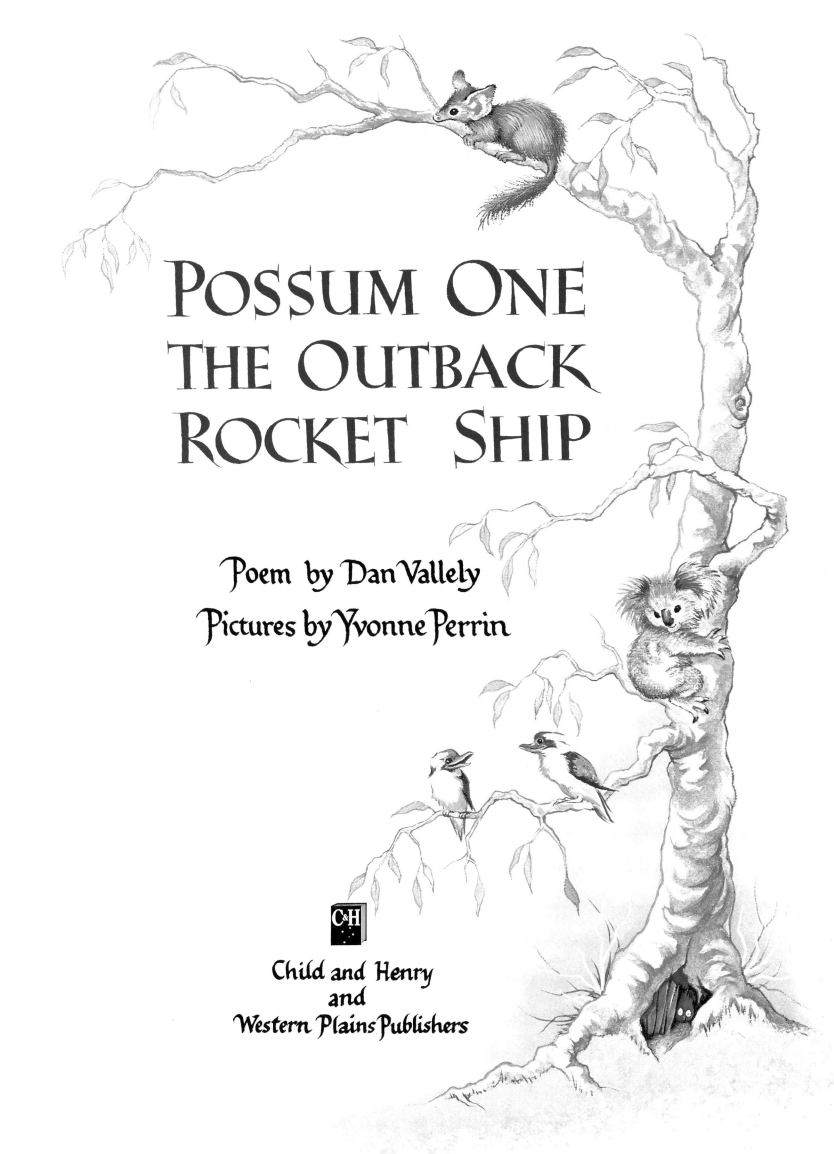

Possum One
The Outback
Rocket Ship

Poem by Dan Vallely

Pictures by Yvonne Perrin

Child and Henry
and
Western Plains Publishers

It was a Monday afternoon
    on the twenty-third of June
when in Possum Creek a strange event occurred.
Striding into town
    in his mortar-board and gown
came Professor Cockatoo, that learned bird.

Ed Galah who was related,
upon conferring, indicated
that his cousin was the bearer of great news,
which he would gladly tell to all
in the Possum Creek Town Hall,
post-haste for there was little time to lose.

8

POSSUM CREEK
TOWN HALL

Within seconds all were seated
and the Professor warmly greeted
as he rose to get proceedings underway.
"Friends and neighbours," he began,
"I have a most exciting plan
which I will now unfold before you if I may.

"I have built a rocket ship
which will be leaving on a trip
very shortly, but I have a need of you.
A number of your best
must face their greatest test
and volunteer to be my rocket crew."

In an hour the recruits
were putting on their suits,
Wally Wombat, Platypus and Ed Galah,
Big Red Kangaroo
and Peter Possum too,
all bound for some enticing distant star.

They could feel the tension mount
as they began the final count,
two seconds, one and then a mighty roar,
as they rose into the sky
they sighed a nervous sigh
and hoped that they would see their homes once more.

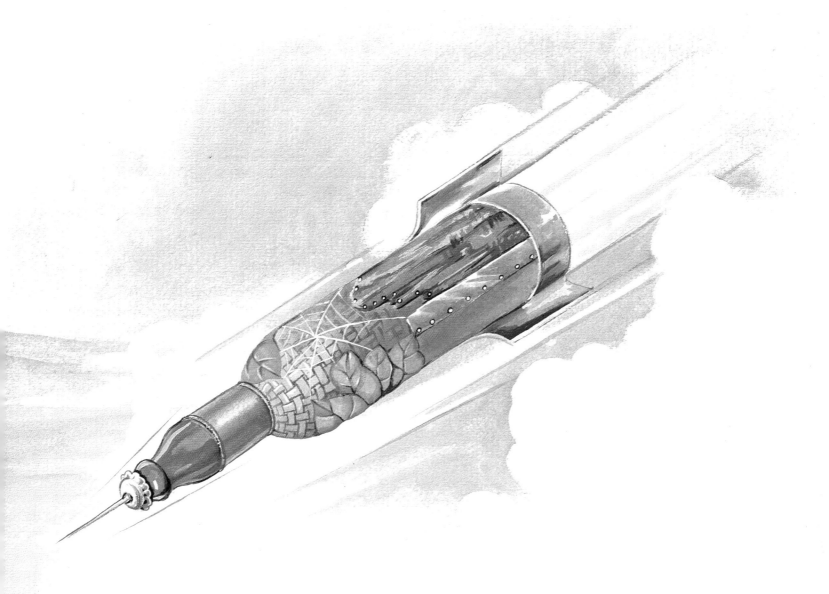

Then with a rolling motion
as if upon an ocean
she veered away from her intended course.
Back towards the ground
she came with dreadful sound
and frightened Tommy Numbat's trotting horse.

Once more on level plane
she roared down Emu Lane
and swept the tiles from Tim Koala's house.
The crew, in disarray,
watched in great dismay
as the wayward rocket chased Marsupial Mouse.

Through the bakery she ploughed
enveloping the crowd
with a coat of flour to everyone's surprise.
And Mrs Tiger Snake
was knocked into the lake
after being struck by several peanut pies.

She screamed left at Dingo Road
and rammed the posh abode
of the Honourable George Goanna, man of leisure,
then carved a gaping path
right through his marble bath
whilst he was in it, much to his displeasure.

On and on she sped,
as the Mayor stood hands on head,
for the only house still standing was his own.
Then her engine coughed and died
and as His Worship cried
she dropped upon his cottage like a stone.

As we came upon the scene
where the Mayoral house had been
the rocket crew were stumbling from the wreck.
With luck that was amazing
injuries were limited to grazing
and a rather minor case of cricked neck.

Thus the saga ended
 in a manner not intended
 and, even though disaster dogged their trip,
 they raised a statue to it
 and the gallant crew who flew it,
        Possum One,
          the Outback
            Rocket Ship.

First Edition 1981
Reprinted 1982
Reprinted 1985

Published by
Child & Henry Publishing Pty Ltd
9 Clearview Place Brookvale, NSW, Australia, 2100
Poems© Dan Vallely 1981
Illustrations © Yvonne Perrin 1981
Printed in Hong Kong
National Library of Australia Card Number and
ISBN 0 86777 168 2